OUR LIBRARY

by EVE BUNTING

Illustrated by MAGGIE SMITH

Clarion Books • New York

To my daughter, Christine,
my favorite librarian
—E.B.

To the Harvard Public Library
in Harvard, Massachusetts—
the lovely little red-brick
library of my childhood
—M.S.

Clarion Books
a Houghton Mifflin Company imprint
215 Park Avenue South, New York, NY 10003
Text copyright © 2008 by Edward D. Bunting
and Anne E. Bunting Family Trust
Illustrations copyright © 2008 by Maggie Smith

The illustrations were executed
in watercolor and acrylic.
The text was set in 15-point Barcelona EF-Book.

www.clarionbooks.com

Printed in Singapore

Library of Congress Cataloging-in-Publication Data
Bunting, Eve, 1928–
Our library / by Eve Bunting ; illustrated by Maggie Smith.
p. cm.
Summary: A raccoon and his friends go to great
lengths to make sure they will always have a
library from which to borrow books.
ISBN-13: 978-0-618-49458-3
ISBN-10: 0-618-49458-8
[1. Libraries—Fiction. 2. Books and reading—Fiction.
3. Raccoons—Fiction. 4. Animals—Fiction.]
I. Smith, Maggie, 1965–, ill.
II. Title.
PZ7.B91527Ot 2007
[E]—dc22 2006009519

TWP 10 9 8 7 6 5 4 3 2 1

Miss Goose stamped my library book. She leaned across her desk. "Our library is going to close forever," she whispered.

"Oh, no!" I said. "Why?"

"It's too old. It needs a new roof. And new paint," Miss Goose said sadly.

"Hmm," I said.

3

We checked out two books.

We read by day, and we read by night.

The next morning, we got started.
We laid a perfect roof.
We painted the library buttercup-yellow,
with sky-blue trim and a grass-green door.

"Beautiful," we said.

"It *is* beautiful," Miss Goose agreed. "But it takes a lot of money to run a library. We don't have a lot of money."

"Hmm," I said.

8

We checked out a book.

We read by day, and we read by night.

Then we had a bake sale,

and an art sale,

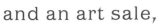

and we sold candy door-to-door.

"Oh, my!" Miss Goose said. "That *is* a lot of money. But Goat owns the ground the library sits on, and he wants it back. He can sell the land for even more money."

We were flummoxed.

"How will we learn without a library?" Mouse asked.

"We'll be ignorant," Skunk said. "And an ignorant skunk is a very sad skunk indeed."

"Hmm," I said. "Remember that it's the library we love—not the land it sits on. Let's find a book."

How to MOVE from ONE PLACE to ANOTHER

We read by day, and we read by night.

And then we looked for the perfect place for our library.

14

"We're going to move it to Buttercup Meadow," we told Miss Goose.

"Oh, my!" she said. "Old Beaver owns Buttercup Meadow. He's a grumpy fellow, and he won't want to give up that meadow. His little grandson plays there every day."

I rubbed my chin. "Hmm! You say he has a little grandson?"
Then and there we checked out two books.

Read to Your GRANDKIDS

HOW TO SPEAK WISELY & WELL to Grumpy Old Beavers

NEW & Updated

We read by day, and we read by night. We looked at the pictures. We thought hard.

Then we went to see Old Beaver in his lodge on Puddle Pond.

"What do you want?" he asked. He was grumpy all right.

Rabbit turned tail and ran.

But I spoke up, wisely and well.

"Sir," I said. "The library is closing. We would like to move it to your beautiful meadow."

"No," Old Beaver grunted, grumpier than ever.

"We know you have a grandson," I went on.
I was fearful but determined. "Where will he
get books to read?"

"With books to read, he'll grow up smart,"
Skunk said.

"And interesting," Squirrel added.

"He'll have fun," I told Old Beaver. "And
reading is something that grandparents and
grandchildren can do together."

"Hmm!" Old Beaver said.

I opened the book I'd brought. "Look!"

Old Beaver peered at the picture. "Those are ducks," he said.

"A grandfather duck and his grandson," I said. "And here is a baby chipmunk with his grandma."

Old Beaver scowled. "No beavers?"

"Not yet," I told him, thinking quickly. "We could send a picture to the publisher."

We waited. Old Beaver slapped the deck
with his broad, flat tail.

We waited some more.

At last, he smiled.
"Oh, all right," he said. "Let me get my
grandson so we can take a picture."

The next day, all of us and some grownups, too,

got together and moved the library.

Our library now sits in the meadow. Buttercups drift around its buttercup-yellow walls. Its grass-green door is always open, and the sky above it is mostly sky-blue.

On rainy days, we stay cozy inside.

On sunny days, we lie in the shade of a big whispering oak tree and read.

OPEN

We have story hour, and parents bring their little ones. Old Beaver and his grandson come in the afternoon, after they've had their naps. They look so content together.

Mole has taken lots of pictures of them.

And Miss Goose has found several books about beavers for the library.

Starting to READ When You've Never READ Before

Badger didn't know how to read, so we're teaching him.

Gopher lies on the grass and kicks up his legs. "There's nothing you can't learn to do when you have books," he says.

Porcupine smoothes down her quills. "If you can read," she adds.

I smile. "And it's even better
if you have a library."